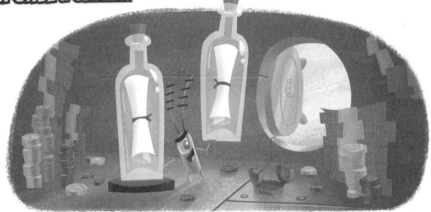

# Krabby Patty Caper

Based on the original screenplay by Stephen Hillenburg,
Paul Tibbitt, Jonathan Aibel, and Glen Berger

Adapted by Mary Tillworth • Illustrated by Caleb Meurer

 **A GOLDEN BOOK • NEW YORK**

© 2015 Paramount Pictures and Viacom International Inc. All rights reserved.
Published in the United States by Golden Books, an imprint of Random House Children's Books,
a division of Random House LLC, 1745 Broadway, New York, NY 10019, and in Canada by
Random House of Canada Limited, Toronto, Penguin Random House Companies. Golden Books,
A Golden Book, A Little Golden Book, the G colophon, and the distinctive gold spine are registered
trademarks of Random House LLC. Nickelodeon, SpongeBob SquarePants, and all related titles, logos,
and characters are trademarks of Viacom International Inc.

created by

*Stephen Hillenburg*

T#: 311423

randomhousekids.com

ISBN 978-0-553-49775-5

Printed in the United States of America    10 9 8 7 6 5 4 3 2 1

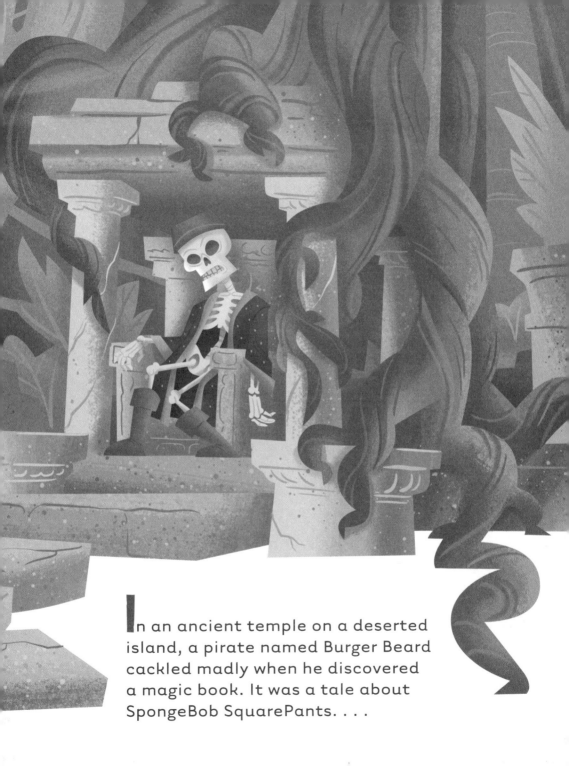

In an ancient temple on a deserted island, a pirate named Burger Beard cackled madly when he discovered a magic book. It was a tale about SpongeBob SquarePants. . . .

It was a sunny morning in Bikini Bottom, and the Krusty Krab was about to open.

SpongeBob and Patrick were in the
kitchen. SpongeBob was ready to flip
some Krabby Patties!

Suddenly, a plane zoomed overhead.
The pilot was Plankton. He was out to
steal the Krabby Patty formula!

"To yer battle stations!" yelled Mr. Krabs.
SpongeBob and Patrick rushed to the roof.
They stopped Plankton with potatoes!

But Plankton had a tank!
SpongeBob squirted ketchup and mustard at
the tank while Patrick threw a jar of mayo. *Boom!*

Plankton rose from the tank wearing a giant robot suit. He stomped on SpongeBob, crashed into the Krusty Krab, cornered Mr. Krabs . . . and froze. The suit was out of gas!

Plankton climbed out of his robot suit.

"Well, Krabs, I guess you've won. I'm down to my last cent trying to put you out of business. You might as well have it."

Plankton tossed a penny to Mr. Krabs. He left, sobbing, as Mr. Krabs put the penny in his safe.

But the sobbing Plankton was a tiny robot. The real Plankton was hiding inside the penny! He grabbed the real formula and quickly replaced it with a fake one.

SpongeBob came into the office and spotted Plankton with the formula.

"Gimme that!" he shouted.

Plankton and SpongeBob fought over the formula, yanking it back and forth. Suddenly, it vanished!

Mr. Krabs blamed Plankton for the formula's disappearance. "Where's me formuler?" he demanded. He lifted his foot to stomp on Plankton.

"Stop!" cried SpongeBob. He pulled out a bottle of bubbles and blew a bubble around Plankton, then hopped inside.

"He doesn't deserve to be crushed for something he didn't do," SpongeBob said, and the bubble floated away.

Without the Krabby Patty formula—and without Krabby Patties—the citizens of Bikini Bottom turned into a hungry, angry mob. Bikini Bottom became a very dangerous place.

SpongeBob peered down at the scene. "We really need to get that formula back."

"What do we do now?" Plankton asked.

"We work together!" declared SpongeBob. "You know, teamwork!"

Plankton frowned. "What's a *tee-am* . . . work?"

"It's easy!" SpongeBob said. "It means I help you and you help me!"

Plankton and SpongeBob decided to build a time machine and grab the formula before it disappeared. They gathered all the parts they needed and got to work.

"I did it!" Plankton said when they had finished.
SpongeBob shook his head. "No, *we* did it!"
Plankton nodded. "We did do it . . . as a *tee-am*!"

Plankton and SpongeBob traveled back in
time to the moment when their past selves
were fighting over the Krabby Patty formula.

They jumped in and wrestled with themselves!
Working as a team, they got the formula back.
Then they hopped into their time machine.

SpongeBob and Plankton time-traveled to the present. Plankton handed the formula to Mr. Krabs. "Here you go, Krabs. She's all yours."

Mr. Krabs opened the bottle. "'Ɛat my subaquatic bubbles,'" he read. SpongeBob and Plankton had grabbed the fake formula!

Just then, a delicious aroma wafted through the air. It smelled like a Krabby Patty!

SpongeBob and his friends followed their noses to a
burger mobile. There they found Burger Beard, who had
used his magic book to steal the Krabby Patty recipe!

SpongeBob realized that everything written in the book would come true! Thinking quickly, he jotted a few lines.

SpongeBob turned his friends into superheroes! Working together, they battled Burger Beard for the formula.

SpongeBob blew a blizzard of bubbles at
Burger Beard, trapping him.
A superhero-sized Plankton picked up the
pirate. "The formula, please," he demanded.

"Team up with me, and we'll be rich and powerful!" Burger Beard said.

Plankton shook his head. "No thanks. I'm already part of a *tee-am* . . . work."

Plankton handed the Krabby Patty formula back to Mr. Krabs.

"Now I realize that keeping something to myself is . . . selfish."

SpongeBob smiled proudly. "Especially when that something is a Krabby Patty!"